This Little Tiger book
belongs to:

_____

_____

_____

For Liz, who loves owls ~ C P

To my uncle Edvard Kristensen ~ T M

LITTLE TIGER PRESS
1 The Coda Centre, 189 Munster Road, London SW6 6AW
www.littletiger.co.uk

First published in Great Britain 2008
This edition published 2015

Text copyright © Caroline Pitcher 2008
Illustrations copyright © Tina Macnaughton 2008
Caroline Pitcher and Tina Macnaughton have asserted their rights
to be identified as the author and illustrator of this work under the
Copyright, Designs and Patents Act, 1988

Printed in China • LTP/1900/1375/1115

4 6 8 10 9 7 5 3

The Littlest Owl

Caroline Pitcher   Tina Macnaughton

LITTLE TIGER PRESS
London

Deep inside a willow tree
were four white eggs.

One egg hatched,
then two, then three,
deep inside a willow tree.

Three owlets blinked at the last white egg.

One said, "It's very quiet in there."

Two said, "Maybe the baby can't get out?"

Three said, "Maybe the egg is empty.

Maybe there isn't a baby inside."

"There is, kee-yooo, there's me,
there's me!" cried the last owlet,
struggling free.
      And there sat Four, so dumpy
and small, a downy white ball.

Deep inside the willow tree, feeding time was such a scrum. One, Two and Three snatched the food. They gobbled and gulped and blinked at Four.

One said, "Oh dear. He's dumpy."

Two said, "Oh dear. He's so small."

Three said, "He'll never grow big and strong like us."

"I will!" cried Four. "Just wait and see."

He scrabbled around in the bottom of the nest, and found a worm for his tea.

One, Two and Three grew more each day.
They jostled and trampled Four, so dumpy
and small, the downy white ball.

Mother Owl hooted, "Don't squash
him, please!"

"I'm fine, Ma," he chirped. "I don't mind
being small at all."

One, Two and Three were changing
fast. They shuffled out on to a branch.
They stretched their wings and
launched themselves into the air.
There they fluttered to and fro,
as soft as moths around the tree.

Four called, "I'll fly too,
kee-yooo, kee-yooo."

Four hopped up and down along the branch. He spread his short wings wide and cried, "Wait for me. I'm coming with you!"

But Four couldn't fly, however hard he tried.

All night long
    Four bobbed and bounced. All day long he fluttered
       and flapped. "I will fly," he cried. "I will! I will!"
          But he never even left the branch.
             When dusk fell,
             Four crept back inside
             the tree and tumbled
             into sleep.

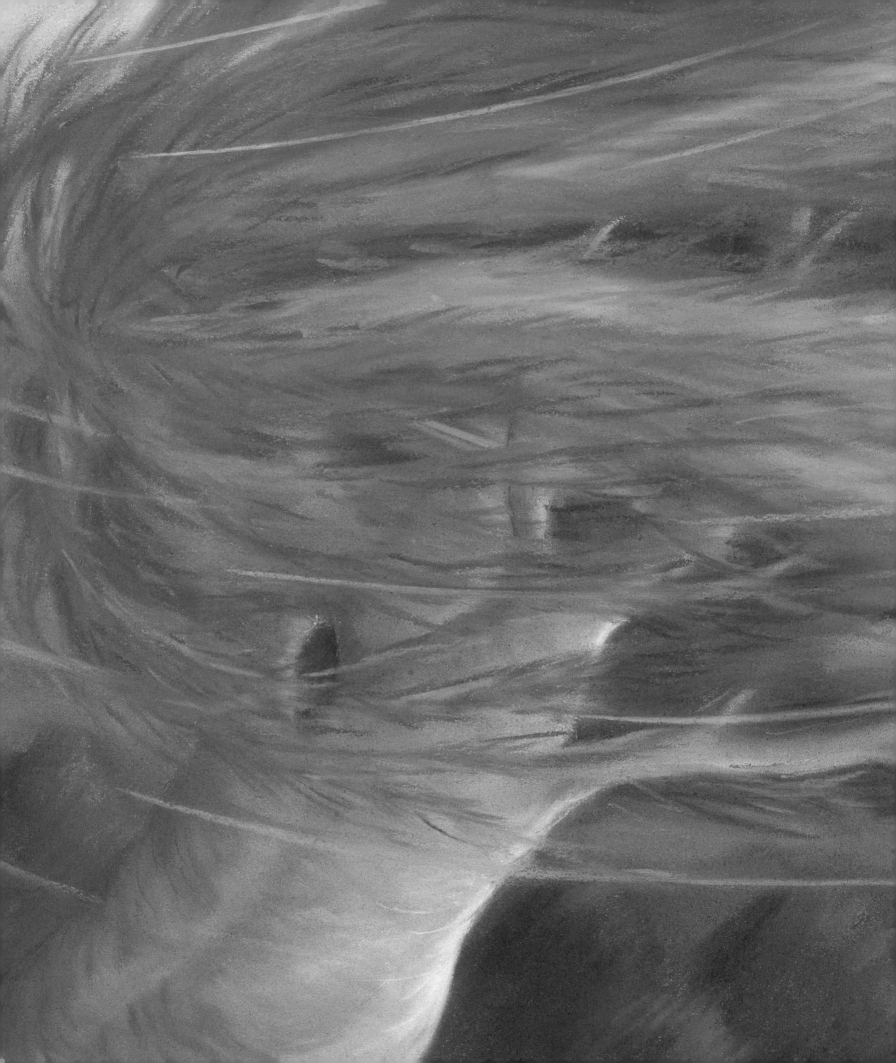

Deep inside the willow tree the owlets
snuggled up and slept. But in the woods the
wind rose up. It gathered together a terrible
storm. It whirled around the willow tree.
The tree was old. It groaned. It creaked.

"Wake up, wake up!" screeched
   Mother Owl. "The willow tree will crack in two!"
   The sleepy owlets struggled out. One by one they
leapt and flew, and battled with the raging wind.
   "Come quickly, Four!" cried One.
   "What if he blows away?" cried Two.
   "What if he still can't fly?" cried Three.

The wind blew Four's downy feathers flat.
It bounced him like a small white ball and tried
to push him from the tree.

He stretched and strained, and flapped and
cried, "I will do it too, kee-yooo. Yes, I'm last
and very small. But I'll never give up at all."

He hurled himself high into the air . . .

. . . and he flew
and flew
and flew!